I LOVE you FOR YOU

Written by
HEATHER LESTER

Illustrated by
VICKY FIELDHOUSE

For Good Media
Lasting Inspiration
CINCINNATI, OHIO

When you came into my life,

I thought I'd teach you to be just like me.

As you've grown I've come to realize,

you have your own unique personality.

You like to wake up early.

I like to sleep in late.

We are different in this way,
but I'll always be your breakfast date.

You like to go slow and explore.

I like to get places fast.

We are different in this way,
but we always have a blast.

You like to dress in bright colors.

I like a more basic style.

We are different in this way,

but your outfits make me smile.

You like to play in trees.

I like my feet on the ground.

We are different in this way,
but if you need me I'll be around.

You like art that is messy.

I like to paint things neat.

We are different in this way,
but you're creating something sweet.

You like to talk every minute of the day.

I like to be as concise as I can be.

We are different in this way,

but what you say is important to me.

Mom,
thanks for the ice
cream. I love you. Do you know
that this is the second time I've
had ice cream today? Sam gave us ice
cream at school for his birthday. Sam also
brought in stickers for everyone. I wanted
the unicorn stickers, but there weren't enough,
so I got the cat stickers. But do you know what
happened? Claire saw that I was sad and she
gave me one of her unicorn stickers. She is so nice.
I gave her one of my cat stickers. Can she come
over and play some time? Look at that bird
over there. I wonder what it would be like to
be a bird. You know how I always say that
I wish I could fly like a bird? What do
you think birds wish for? Do you
think they wish to be people?
Can we bring some
shells home
today?

You like books with
dragons and wizards.

I like to zip through
mysteries with speed.

We are different in this way,
but I'll always sit with you and read.

You like to perform with a band.

I like to be in the crowd.

We are different in this way,

but you make me so proud.

You like to get dirty.

I like to stay clean.

We are different in this way,

but on me you can always lean.

Sometimes you get mad.

Sometimes

I might

shout.

Sometimes we see things differently,

but we will work it out.

My child,
we are different,

but this I know
is true...

You be who you're
meant to be,

and I'll love you for you.

To Dustin, Sophia, Nathan, and Caroline - H.L.

To Neil and Leo - V.F.

For Good Media
Lasting Inspiration

Published by For Good Media, LLC
Cincinnati, Ohio
www.forgoodmedia.com

Text © 2017 Heather Lester
Illustrations © 2017 Vicky Fieldhouse
Editing by Tanya Jones
All rights reserved

Library of Congress Control Number: 2017918415

Hardback ISBN: 978-0-9992621-0-8
Paperback ISBN: 978-0-9992621-1-5
Printed in the USA

First Edition, 2018
10 9 8 7 6 5 4 3 2 1